VENGEFUL HANK

AND OTHER SHORTWEIRD STORIES

VENGEFUL HANK

AND OTHER SHORTWEIRD STORIES

MARCEL ST. PIERRE

Copyright © Marcel St. Pierre 2016

Published by MKZ Press

All rights reserved

The use of any part of this publication reproduced, transmitted in any form or by any means, electronic, mechanical, photocopying, recording, or otherwise, or stored in a retrieval system, without the prior written consent of the publisher—or, in case of photocopying or other reprographic copying, a licence from the Canadian Copyright Licensing Agency—is an infringement of the copyright law.

Issued in print and electronic formats

ISBN 978-0-9949409-2-6 (bound)
ISBN 978-0-9949409-3-3 (Kindle)

Cover design © Marcel St. Pierre

MKZ Press
2538 Waterford Street
Oakville, Ontario, Canada L6L 5E7
mkzpress@mkz.com

Table of Contents

Beforeword 9
Foreword 11
Afterword 13
Moreword 15
Dedication 17
Magoffin's Red Button 19
Clorph the Elder & His Gravity Diapers 21
Straw Men in Straw Hats 23
Le Triangle Bermuda 25
Waking Moments 27
Newton's Wrath upon the Apple Tree 29
The Therapy of Jurisprudence 31
That Time I Met Bill Murray 33
Random & Simka 35
Clompus Skips a Stone .37
The Fog 41
Hammer of the Gods 43
The Interview 45
Caveman at the Large Hadron Collider 47
Eggs in the Microwave .51
This Looks Like 53
A Different Banana 55
Perch, Broccoli & Wild Rice 57
The Victoria County Dominion Day Pie Eating
Contest, 1904 59
Thrünkle Heyerdäöl Opens the Fridge 61

Thunder & Heebly Make It Right	63
Mandrake by Moonlight	65
The Birdperson of Corktown	67
Vengeful Hank	71
The Man-Corset	73
Mark Twain	75
Deep and Delicious	77
I Know What I Know	79
The Bishop & the Fairy	81
A Hint of Mint	83
Long Weekend	85
The Deceased	87
Hitchhiker Games	89
Oven Exam	91
Afterlife Wishes	93
Karl	95
The Last Visit	97
Sullen Artists	99
Two Roads Diverged in a Yellow Wood	101
The Antique Sink	103
Torquil's Cheddar	105
Defensive Driving	107
The Five Badgers of Skip Stephenson	109
Inspector Withersby Strikes Again	111
The Raven, Part II	113
Death	117
Fiddler Crab in the Top Hat	119
Knobby Retires	121

What Do You See?	125
The Homonym Strangler	129
Fruit Bat Pie	133
Just Desserts	137
Late Night Diner	141
The Last One	143
Acknowledgements	147
About the Author	149

Beforeword

You will scratch your head. You will say what the—? You will get it... or possibly not. But you will laugh at these strange vignettes... you will enjoy the off-beat linguistic romp, the surprise and the delightful twists. These are sketches of a sunshine mind making leaps of logic into the absurd.

Sheree Fitch
Author of Kiss The Joy As It Flies
Stephen Leacock Award for
Literary Humour shortlist

Foreword

It's easy to tell people "I know Marcel". But when you actually have to write it down, and you know it will be in a book, and you have to sign your name at the bottom like some kind of legal document, well, the little voice in my head cautions me "do you really want to put in writing that you know him?"

I push myself away from my desk. Take a deep breath and read nine shortweird stories. They are very clever. Like Marcel. Weird. Like Marcel. They are short too. Like Marcel as well. After some pacing and several bowls of cereal I decide that I will write; I know Marcel, I think he is funny and I like his stories. I like this approach. I'm not being specific as to what exactly I find funny about him.

The stories I like don't have to be the ones in

this book. Maybe they're stories he's told me over lunch. Though, having now just read eight more, I really *do* like these shortweird stories. I charge on. I need to wrap up this foreword. Perhaps tell a warm Marcel anecdote that tugs at a few heartstrings. Something that confirms Marcel is a nice guy. A clever performer. A funny improvisor. And now an author?

Oh, screw it. I don't care what the little voice in my head says. Marcel St Pierre is a lovely man. Sure he has a French name, but you wouldn't know it if you met him. I know him. I like him and I'm damn proud of it.

Peter Wildman
Actor, writer, comedian
Founding member of The Frantics

Afterword

Marcel St. Pierre's short weird stories are definitely short. And weird. But they're also a lot more. They're funny, charming, surprising, whimsical—it's hard to find the right words to describe how much of a delight they are. Each is an imaginative gem where what's real is redefined and the absurd has become the new normal. I couldn't stop smiling from the moment I picked them up. The stories are really fun to read. And why not? They're short. And weird.

Don Ferguson
Actor, Writer, Comedian, Author
Founding member of
The Royal Canadian Air Farce

Moreword

Marcel St. Pierre's collection of short stories is called Vengeful Hank and Other Shortweird Stories. Never has a title of a book so correctly advertised what is between the covers.

Whether it's the tale of Clorph The Elder, whose yoghurt filled diapers hope to defy gravity, or the account of the aftermath of Isaac Newton's encounter with an apple, or any other of the stories within, you will never find more definitive examples of weird. And, as advertised, each story is literally short, one paragraph, one page at the longest.

I laughed, ate a sandwich, laughed again, worried about Marcel for a while, then laughed again. Read!

Colin Mochrie,
Actor, producer, improvisor
Author of Not Quite The Classics

Dedication

For Leah. I love you.

I love how you laugh at things I say, even if I'm not trying to be funny. I also love those times when I say something I think is extremely funny and you don't laugh.

Because it's the little things.

Magoffin's Red Button

Magoffin's finger hovered over the red button for the hidden trap door that lay just in front of his antique mahogany desk. His visitor was—as usual—a bespectacled yellow penguin riding a unicycle and wearing a jumbo shrimp for a hat.

Usually his be-wheeled visitors simply rolled in and sat there, their sad eyes silently staring at him just above desk level, until he lost patience or interest. But today, he felt hesitant about sending his guest plunging to certain doom.

He couldn't be sure, but Magoffin thought he'd just heard this particular penguin speak. And if that was so, then it had just uttered the words "no button, please." That, or maybe it had said "walnut puppies."

"Either way," thought Magoffin, "Penguin's got balls."

Clorph the Elder & His Gravity Diapers

"If my theory is right," Clorph The Elder yelled to his son below, "These yoghurt-filled diapers I'm wearing will defy gravity!" And with that, Clorph threw himself from the ramparts.

Of course, he was wrong about the gravity-defying properties of his yoghurt-filled diapers, having failed to comprehend, instead, their wormhole-creating properties. Rather than defy gravity, he accelerated sideways into the gaping, toothy maw of a Scolerian crunge beast that materialized in the sky.

And today, "Clorph the Younger's Travelling Freakshow" has a Scolerian crunge beast that most people think is just a fat goat with fake wings and a lisp.

Straw Men in Straw Hats

"Good day," said Timothy Festoon to the bank teller. As he turned to leave the counter at the Savings & Loan, someone stood in his way. It was his arch nemesis, Calhoun O'Malley.

"Good day to you, sir!" harrumphed O'Malley, moustache twitching, refusing to give Festoon the right of way. Everyone in the cue sighed in breathless anticipation. The Festoon-O'Malley rivalry was legendary, stemming from some long-forgotten slight that neither family could prove had ever actually happened.

"I said, good *day*, sir!" huffed Festoon. He would certainly not give way to O'Malley, if it was the last thing he did.

"Yes, *good day!*" puffed O'Malley, steadfast in his intention to force Festoon back through the cue, forcing him to excuse himself to every client in line, like an idiot, before making his way out the door.

"Good day to *you*, sir!" countered Festoon, determined to force O'Malley to acquiesce, as any sane, normal person would.

"*Good day, sir!*" frothed O'Malley, who was neither sane or normal.

"Sir, I said good *day!*"

"Good day to *you*, sir!"

With each valediction bade, the two closed ground on each other. Toe to toe, nose to nose, spittle to whisker they invaded each other's personal space, each doggedly wishing the other an aggressive, insincere, and hopefully final adieu.

"*Good day!*"

"I am the one who shall bid *you* a good day, sir."

"You are in error, for it is I who shall bid *you* a good day, from today until the end of days, *sir*, and I use that term *lightly*."

"*Good day!*"

"Indeed, *good day* to you!"

"I said *good day*, sir!"

Then an albino tiger riding a wendigo shot and ate them, because life was simpler in the 1920s.

Le Triangle Bermuda

As he did whenever he wanted their attention, Capitaine Fromage shot one of his crew with his pistol.

"Alors, mateys," said the Capitaine. "Fermez la bouche! Je comprend there is some mutinous parlez-vous since we entered le mists de le Triangle Bermuda? Vous pensez I have been acting mal à la tête? Hein? C'est vrai?"

The crew muttered to themselves. "Well," continued the Capitaine. "Parlez-vouz?! Qui est le malaise?"

First mate Stumpy cleared his throat. "Well, sir," he began.

"Oui?" said Capitaine, impatiently.

"When did you become French, sir?"

Capitaine was aghast. "Mais what?!? When did je...? Est-ce que je not always been French?"

Shrugs, a "not really" and some "I-don't-knows" were the crew's reply. "Did we not dine on vichyssoise ce matin? Is this ship non pas Le Black Patisserie?!?!"

The crew all shrugged, remembering rather that the ship had been named The Black Horse, before "someone" had recently painted over the word "horse" with white paint. "Well, to be honest, sir..." began Stumpy.

"That's mon-sir to vous! *Voulez-vous la guilloutine?!?*" continued the Capitaine.

"No," said the crew listlessly, defeated.

"Non, *qui!?!?*"

"Non, Capitaine Fromage..." sighed the crew. At that point, the Capitaine's fake moustache fell off.

"J'accuse!!!" he screamed, firing blindly into their midst, as their ship sailed away into the thickening fog.

Waking Moments

Darkness faded to the dim light of dawn as Michael's sleep-encrusted eyes slowly cracked open. Consciousnesses trickled into his mind, like the drip of a percolator, but what flowed into the cup of his brain that morning was not coffee. It was the sound of quiet, blubbering sobs.

For Michael could hear the thoughts of pickles.

And from the kitchen, at the bottom of a jar in the fridge – a lonely and inconsolable gherkin remembered his friends and waited for the light.

Newton's Wrath upon the Apple Tree

"We are all well-versed in the story of how the apple fell on Isaac Newton's head, which led him to theorize the existence of gravity," began Professor Gnornebonge, peering at his first-year physics class over his horn-rims.

"But, who here knows," he continued, "that in the forgotten moments immediately post said apple falling, that Sir Newton - in a fit of rage - shot the tree multiple times with his musket, stabbed it with a sword, set fire to it and then ordered his servants to cut it down?"

All the students shook their heads, except for the apple tree in the front row who raised a branch in acknowledgement. The class shifted uncomfortably in a collective, quiet shame.

The Therapy of Jurisprudence

"And so, Doctor Syzzlk," said Jurisprudence, "This is why I'm convinced that inside my cupboard... is a bear!" at which point she screamed.

"A bear?" asked Syzzlk. Jurisprudence screamed in fright again. "Yes," she stammered, tears spraying from her eyes.

"I see," said the Doctor as he cleaned his glasses with a large squeegee. "And do you see a pattern in these... behaviours?"

"Behaviours?"

"Yes. In our sessions, you've stated various phobias with a common theme. You're afraid of pears, bears, chairs, stairs and squares," he said, pausing each time Jurisprudence screamed at an item in the list.

"And Fred Astaire," she reminded him, then screamed, having frightened herself.

"It is my professional opinion," he said,

"That you are afraid of anything that rhymes with the word 'air'." She screamed. "Do you see the connection?" he asked.

"Au contraire," she screamed, bursting several blood vessels in her right eye, so sudden and complete was her fright and the will to express it. Out of ideas, the doctor then reached across the room with his tentacles to strangle her.

The moral of the story? Beware the Octopsychologist! For he is no substitute for proper therapy!

That Time I Met Bill Murray

I was filling up with unleaded last night when, to my surprise, Bill Murray got into my passenger seat.

"I've got no time to explain," he yelled at me through the open window, "Just get in!"

I opened the driver's door and was about to say something (and maybe get a selfie) when Margaret Cho materialized in the front seat. She shot Bill with a taser, then punched me in the throat. As I doubled over, she chanted some weird incantation, and the whole car suddenly shot straight up into the sky till it was just a speck, and then, gone.

"You still gotta pay for that gas," said the attendant, watching me gasping for breath. "And I didn't see nothin'."

Random & Simka

Random and Simka were on the roof again, bundled up in layers and a blanket as they shared sips from a bottle of scotch. It got dark early at this time of year, and though it was barely six p.m., dusk had already smudged its way across the horizon, and the city lights began their night's work of snuffing out most of the twinkle from the evening sky.

"What do you think is gonna happen?" asked Simka.

"I think he's gonna get elected again." said Random.

"You do?"

"Yip."

"That sucks."

"So does he," said Random, taking another small swig. "But people get what they deserve, I guess."

"Why do you say that?" asked Simka.

"A lot of people don't vote anyway. So that's basically the same as telling everybody to just go ahead and make the decision," replied Random. "And not enough people who didn't want him there in the first place voted at all, if they'd paid any attention or really cared."

"So, apathy, then," said Simka, offering Random the last bit of scotch.

"Apathy," replied Random, waving off the bottle. "You finish it."

They cuddled closer under the blanket as she took the last swig. "I feel bad for his family," she said.

"Me, too..." he said. "But they don't really care about us, because he doesn't either."

They sat in silence for a few moments. In the distance, police sirens could be heard, and Simka looked in that direction. "I guess that's them."

"I guess it is," said Random.

"Should we go downstairs?"

"Nah. They'll find us," he said. "It's nice out here."

And there they stayed. And the police did soon find them, and had many questions about the naked, duct-taped and intoxication politician they'd just found in their apartment. They were going to be famous.

Clompus Skips a Stone

Clompus Flangcks was a simple man who lived his life according to simple rules. He lived in the moment, and he'd spent many moments this particular morning walking along the beach to find a perfectly round stone, just the right size and shape to skip out into the ocean.

"I want a stone that is neither pumice nor quartz," he said aloud to all the stones at his feet. "For pumice is too airy, and quartz too reflective. Also, I need a stone no larger than the palm of my hand, the better for me to wrap my fingers and thumb around to throw it."

He was going to throw this stone as hard as he could and, as far as he misunderstood the physics involved, it would travel in a straight line until the actual gravity of the earth pulled it down, in free fall, causing the rock to travel around the earth, right back to his hand.

But then a thought struck him. "What if

that's not how physics works? What if I throw this stone so hard it simply flies straight out into space? How can it return if it is travelling forever in a straight line?"

He stood still, puzzling over this for nearly three hours, till he came to believe that the universe was almost like a tunnel in Pac Man. That is to say, if he threw this stone in enough of a straight line in one direction, it would travel to the end of the cosmos and would obviously reappear behind him, and then he would catch it.

He found the perfect stone.

He kissed the stone, which surprised them both.

He threw it.

It fell into the ocean about forty feet away.

Clompus was puzzled. He assumed he hadn't thrown the stone hard enough. Still, this was easy to fix. First, all he needed to do was lift up the ocean to find his stone. He spent his final years on Earth going down to the beach, every morning, vainly trying to grab a handful of ocean and lift it up like a blanket.

Meanwhile, the stone itself sat forty feet away under the ocean and sulked. It had spent nearly twelve million years getting to that spot on the beach where Clompus had found him, only to be thrown back a thousand years. The sheer inconsiderate inconvenience of the act bred within the stone a great resentment.

The earth kept turning for another five billion years, till the day the sun exploded. By some impossibly complex, mathematically-impossible fluke of statistical improbability, the stone was flung out into the far reaches of space, the only surviving physical relic of our planet.

An unknowable amount of moments later, the stone was found adrift by a race of alien scientists from a planet named Richard. After studying all the scorched and ancient Earthly DNA strands burnt into its surface, one of Richard's most famous scientists–let's call him Richard, too - came to believe the stone to be sentient. He believed there must be way of communicating with it. Nobody on Richard believed Richard could do it. But Richard of Richard did it.

The sentient stone learned the language of the people of Richard.

The stone became a politician and was elected to Richard's highest office.

After solving all of Richard's political, social, economic and extra-marital problems, the stone enlisted all of Richard's brightest minds; and within millennia, the Richards had evolved into a society of near God-like beings, masters of time, space and dimension, till they fused into a single, giant knowledge cloud known as Caitlyn Jenner.

The stone knew the time had now come for Caitlyn Jenner to fling him backwards through time, back to a past probable Earth. And so they did, and so it was that the stone re-entered Earth's atmosphere, trailing a plume of fire a kilometer long, at the exact moment before Clompus had thrown him into the ocean.

The force of impact vaporized Clompus, the stone, and much of the eastern seaboard of North America.

"Because fuck that guy," thought the stone, as non-existence claimed him, finally and eternally.

The Fog

Had he been paddling for five minutes or five hours? Hilding didn't know any more, but he knew he had to be somewhere to be... or was it not be..?

He became aware of his breathing, the lapping waves... and faint sitar music? And then... out of the fog... he saw a shadow... faintly at first, then more distinct...

And he found himself staring open-mouthed at another boat with another Hilding in it, staring back at him open-mouthed as their boats floated past each other.

Kaboom! Pow! And then, he was standing in his kitchen, disoriented, naked and painted blue, holding an open jar with nothing but the words 'Holy Fuck Peppers' on the label.

Hammer of the Gods

Long ago, high over the village of Hnyørk, fingers of lightning and a single thunderclap heralded the arrival of a cylinder that dropped, screaming and smoking from the sky, into the village pigsty.

No one knew exactly what to make of it. Made of the finest, brightest metal that surely no human blacksmith had forged, none could make sense of the strange markings on its side that read LOCKHEED X12. Still, all were thankful that, despite their great fear and squealing, not a single pig had been lost.

For days the strange object sat there, cooled and washed by the rain, until smoke no longer issued from it.

It was decided that no-one wanted to be around when the owners of this object – surely Gods – came round to reclaim it. It was impossible to reason with the Gods when they thought you'd stolen something they themselves had misplaced, so arrangements were made to relocate the entire village to the other side of the fjord.

But on the night before the migration was to start, Erik Sorenson, the village tinker, had a dream. He dreamt of a longboat full of the village men, travelling a great distance to a new world in a very short time-span, propelled by a metal forge of fire spewing a great flame from its stern.

He woke in a sweaty fit. The Gods had given him a vision, and he got up straight away and went to his stables. The dawn found him with his horses, hauling the obelisk out of the pigsty and into his shop.

There was a great hue and cry from all the villagers, and great dissent among the elders, but Erik told them of his vision, convinced it was the Gods of Asgard themselves who had given it to him. "The Gods help those who help themselves," he told them. "Surely it is they who dropped the object in the village pigsty on purpose, no matter how inconveniently placed it might be."

But this is not the story of how Erik spent the next four years tinkering with attaching an experimental jet engine from another dimension to a Viking longboat. This is the story of Grynker Vålvœ, sole survivor of Erik's crew, who begged in vain for Erik to indulge him and let him equip the longboat on its maiden voyage with his new invention, a thing he called a "seat belt".

The Interview

Mr. Lyons turned the screen for them both to look at. "Impressive website, Denyse," he said, and he meant it.

"Shank you," replied Denyse, blushing. He was probably old enough to be her Dad, but she thought again how cute he looked.

"I've checked your references and again, very happy with what I've heard," he continued. "I've just got one question. It's a small thing, really, but... well... uh... I just have to ask you."

"Yesh?"

Lyons took his glasses off and rubbed his nose. "Are you..." he trailed off and cleared his throat. "Are you a human-sized chipmunk wearing spaghetti for hair?"

"Um..." Denyse began, furtively picking up his smart-phone and shoving it into her bulging cheek pouch. "Yesh."

"I see." Lyons nodded. "Can you start Monday?"

Caveman at the Large Hadron Collider

The media was going wild; scientists at the Large Hadron Collider had gone public to address a bizarre event at the 27-kilometre tunnel facility located under the Franco-Swiss border.

For days, there had been rumours of a gibbering caveman who'd appeared on the site, clubbing scientists in the cafeteria and eating their food, before shuffling away to hide somewhere in the facility. "I can now confirm," said Hadron's official spokesperson, "that this rumour is true."

The murmuring press gallery erupted in questions and camera flashes. The spokesperson's voice raised above the din. "Please, quiet, please."

The room quieted down. "Thank you," he continued. "Now, no harm will come to the caveman," he assured them. "We are in the process of doing a sweep of the facility to locate him and ensure he doesn't hurt himself or cause any further injury to others."

Hands shot up as did voices and tempers from the press gallery "Please," asked the spokesperson, raising his hands. "Please, let me finish. I'm sure you have lots of questions and we'll get to all of those after my statement."

The room quieted down.

"Now, how did this happen in the first place? We believe this caveman is actually a janitor, one Kyle Hernandez, and that he was transformed into this proto-human when he walked through a revolving door while the collider was operating. We believe that as a side-effect of our research experiments here, that we have created the world's first de-volving door. "

Hands, voices and tempers shot again. "Please," asked the spokesperson, raising his hands. "Please, again, let me finish. I'm sure you have lots of questions but I assure you we'll get to all of those after my statement."

The room quieted down.

"Thank you," he continued. "Now. We've yet to determine if this door's properties have practical applications for curing disease, time travel or warp drive, but we should have those answers once we've freed our key creative team from the Hellevator..."

The collective jaws of the world's media dropped in an awkward pause. "Oh, ahh, okay, I see..." continued the Hadron spokesperson, mentally hating himself for the slip-up. "Perhaps I should back up a bit..."

Eggs in the Microwave

On Sunday morning a drowsy Smudge Grant, in t-shirt and pajama bottoms, put several eggs in a bowl of water and put them in the microwave.

"It's not a great idea to make hardboiled eggs in the microwave," said his girlfriend, without looking up from her newspaper. Smudge yawned, ignored her and sipped his coffee.

After a few moments, the microwave beeped, and Smudge opened the door. And that's when a pair of mutated chicken-monster hands burst out, grabbing him by the neck.

Smudge had never screamed like a girl before, but today was a day for new ideas, so scream he did. Finally managing to pry the hands off his neck with a spatula, he forced them back into the microwave and slammed the door shut before collapsing, gasping, on the kitchen floor.

Without looking up from her paper, his girlfriend spoke.

"See?"

This Looks Like

"This looks like angel dandruff," thought Djonathan Cronch as he walked through the snowy woods in the fading light of late afternoon. For the last hour, he'd been playing a childhood game he'd invented to fight off boredom or anxiety.

"This looks like walking through curtains of stars," he thought a moment later. It might not have been the smartest idea to take off for the family cabin in the middle of a snowstorm, but he and Alison hadn't been doing too well lately, and if she was taking a girl's weekend like she wanted, why shouldn't he find a little time for himself to think, alone? The cabin seemed like the perfect place.

He was beginning to regret his decision to leave the car parked when he'd found the secondary side roads leading to the isolated cabin hadn't been plowed. "This looks like travelling through hyperspace," he thought, trying to distract himself from the nagging doubt that he'd gotten himself turned around and lost.

The snow had been plentiful this year, and he was now wading through hip-high snow. Why hadn't he followed the road instead of deciding to trek overland to the cabin?

But it was then that he spotted a familiar landmark; the words "Djon & Ali 4 ever" carved into a tree. Relief came to him then, and just two minutes later, he'd crested a small hill and looked down gratefully at the shape of the cabin through the dusky snow.

"This looks like the place," he thought as he stomped the snow off his boots on the front steps, stuck his key in the lock and swung the door open. The smell of incense, pot and sweat hit him then like a physical thing, and the scene before him seared itself into his eyeballs like the bacon sizzling on the stove.

Inside the smoke-filled cabin were about ten startled, naked old men staring at him, frozen in a variety of incriminatingly kama-sutratic positions. One of them was wearing a goat's head and held a smoldering bong.

Someone coughed uncomfortably.

Then Goat Head spoke up. "This isn't what it looks like," he said. But Djonathan was pretty sure it was.

A Different Banana

Neilson Conroy walked down a long corridor with a clipboard. It was his first day on the new job and he was eager to make a good impression.

He stopped at a tiny shuttered window labeled "#1". Sensors detected his presence, and the shutter lifted. Inside was a banana on a pedestal. The shutter came back down, and he looked at the sheet on his clipboard:

1. What did you just see?

   a) A banana

   b) Different banana

   (c) Other? Fill in blank: _____

He circled (a) and walked to the next window. The shutter went up. Inside he saw a banana.

The second question was the same as the

first, so he circled (b) and continued.

He then peered into the third window. What he saw caused his bowels to empty violently. Other food-like contents and fluids at other digestive stages found other exit orifices. Neilson ran screaming out the exit.

A team of faraway scientists watching Neilson on closed-circuit monitors clucked in disappointment. "This either proves we have to stop hiring through Craigslist, or that's really NOT another banana in there."

Perch, Broccoli & Wild Rice

Farsnard couldn't believe what he was experiencing. For reasons he did not comprehend, the food he had just eaten was somehow... un-eating itself.

He could feel it coming back up his esophagus, could feel it reassembling itself as he chewed (or rather, un-chewed it), could feel it as he brought the fork down from his mouth and un-skewered the food in its original state back onto his plate.

And there it was; a full meal of perch, broccoli and wild rice. And he then walked his plate backwards to the kitchen and placed the food back into the cooking pans, as he proceeded to un-cook his meal.

It was then that he realized that while time was certainly moving backwards, his <u>consciousness</u> was somehow moving forward. What could possibly explain why this was happening?

Nothing, as it turned out. And there was

similarly nothing he could do to stop it.

And so he spent the next 33 years living his life backwards, sunset to sunrise, as he experienced the bliss of un-making his dumb mistakes, the thrill of un-losing money he'd gambled away frivolously, and the ecstasy of backwards orgasms.

It wasn't until he found himself un-eating paste in Grade Four that his forward-moving mind realized that his backwards-moving body was going to eventually go right back up his mother's vagina… and that really kinda buzz-killed the whole thing, right there.

The Victoria County Dominion Day Pie Eating Contest, 1904

Ronnie Muckler had been the Victoria County Dominion Day Pie Eating Contest Champion for a decade. Rhubarb, apple or cherry, Ronnie was king. Blueberry? More like piece-of-cake-berry.

"No human can defeat me," bragged Ronnie, and Victoria County hated braggarts. But this year, no one seemed willing to challenge him, so it was with glee that the organizers accepted a last-minute challenge from Satan, who had just moved into the area from Maine.

When Satan cloven-footedly appeared at the table, Flounder's Park got really quiet. Rules were read, the starting pistol fired, and the filling began to fly.

For six minutes, the opponents were pie for pie. But the rules said nothing about sprouting extra mouths, so when a second pie-hole appeared in the middle of Satan's forehead, Ronnie began sweating.

The rules were also vague about other pie-holes, so when Satan began fisting pie up a certain unmentionable hole with his prehensile tail, Ronnie vomited, slamming his fists down on the table in defeat.

The crowd erupted in cheers, and rushed to lift Satan onto their shoulders in paroxysms of joy. Then, with the town's awful marching band leading the procession, they carried their new Dark Champion down the boulevard to the pit at the end of Manse Street, where they threw him in and poured molten slag over him before sealing it up with a huge stone.

Because Satan never gets a break.

Thrünkle Heyerdäöl Opens the Fridge

Thrünkle Heyerdäöl knew about the rule of thirds.

For instance; the rule of thirds in photography, whereby placing certain points of interest within certain areas of a photograph made them more interesting. He knew the rule of thirds applied to comedy as well, but Thrünkle was unsure what the rule of thirds said about his refrigerator.

He'd opened it twice in the last two minutes to get an egg.

On the first try, his fridge door had opened to reveal the African savannah. A gazelle in the distance had stared straight at him while chewing grass.

Startled, he'd closed the door quickly. Was he having a flashback from something he'd taken in college? By degrees, he convinced himself that of course, he'd hallucinated the whole thing.

When he opened the fridge door the second time, he not only saw the Savannah again, but he noticed the gazelle was much closer now, standing on its hind legs, trying to look innocent as it fumbled to hide a switchblade behind its back.

He shut the door and stood there a while. Understandably, he was unsure about opening the fridge a third time.

Still… he really wanted that egg.

Thunder & Heebly Make It Right

Megabob Thunder stomped on the brakes and squealed to a stop by the side of the road, leaving three 50-foot skid marks behind him. The 1988 Cutlass Supreme would have left four tracks, if not for the fact that the front right wheel was a snowmobile ski.

Hingle Heebly woke from his troubled sleep in the back seat. "What?! What is it?!" he blurted. Megabob looked at Hingle in the rearview, then pointed straight ahead. Over the crest of the next hill, they could see a huge billowing cloud of black smoke. Vultures circled overhead.

Hingle's shoulders sank. "Fuck."

An hour later, they'd walked the rest of the way overland to the top of the hill, from where they could see a farmhouse surrounded by a vineyard. The plume of smoke was coming from behind the house. The vultures still circled overhead, but nothing else was moving anywhere else on the property, as far as they could see.

Under the cover of the overgrown shrubs and bushes, they crept surreptitiously to the side of the house, then snuck along the west side until they could peer around the corner into the back yard.

There they saw a grizzly bear in a shawl and farmer hat pinned under a burning tractor, unable to free himself. He was being prodded and poked with sticks by at least half a dozen foot-tall naked baby dolls painted in various colours.

Megabob looked at Heebly.

Heebly nodded.

Producing sawed-off shotguns from their overcoats, they emerged from the corner of the house. Shoulder to shoulder, they blasted the dolls to pieces with shell after shell as they advanced on the tractor, step by step."

It was over in 25 seconds.

Then, as Thunder collected the doll heads, Heebly rested his gun barrel between the bear's eyes and smiled. "No!" said the bear. "Please. I can't go back there!"

Heebly sighed. "Don't make this harder than it has to be, Jared," he said, sadly. "You're the only scientist bear left."

Mandrake by Moonlight

As he sat in the bay window looking out at the moonlit night, Mandrake smiled to himself. No-one was home yet.

"Good," he thought. "I hate my room-mates anyway. More me time."

He stretched for a moment and yawned. Nighttime was when he did his best thinking, and also his best whatever the fuck he wanted. So he played with his ball of yarn for a while.

Then, without warning, he saw something in the corner of his eye. Every muscle in his body went taut as his head whipped around to see a disembodied spirit floating along the floor, darting behind the couch.

He leapt from his seat and ran over to the couch, bouncing off his favourite cushion and clawing his way up the wall. This knocked down the framed Casablanca poster, shattering the glass as it fell behind the couch. Frightened by the noise, he scrambled onto the kitchen table and sat there, hyperventilating, till little by little, he could breathe again, and he realized something.

"Ha! I'm sitting on the *fucking* kitchen table!" he thought. "I fucking *own* this place!". Then he randomly scampered to the bathroom, where he unrolled a full roll of toilet paper on the floor. Then, arching his back to make himself look larger, he rushed sideways on all fours — down the hallway to the front door — where he barfed in a shoe.

Then he returned to his bay window and started grooming his anus.

"Fuck everybody!" thought Mandrake, who was a 24-year old chartered accountant from Markham, and not a cat.

The Birdperson of Corktown

As Merk got onto the streetcar, he saw The Birdperson again, sitting in the back row, with just one empty seat across from her/him/it. Quickly scanning the crowded car, he saw no other option, and so began the trudge of dread towards his acquaintance.

When he'd first seen The Birdperson on the streetcar a month ago, Merk had given him/her/it a wide berth and pretended he just didn't see it/her/him. And then after a few moments, he'd made eye contact with The Birdperson and smiled, but he/she/it had just stared at him till he felt so uncomfortable, he'd gotten off the streetcar before his stop and walked home, ashamed of himself.

It had bothered him for weeks, but today Merk wanted to be a better person, the person he knew he could be. As The Birdperson tracked him the entire length of the streetcar, Merk avoided eye contact, finally making his way to the seat across from him/it/her.

He sat down in what he hoped seemed a convincingly nonchalant way. The Birdperson kept staring. And just a moment before he felt he surely couldn't continue pretending not to notice, Merk returned its/her/his gaze and nod-smiled, feigning surprise. "Oh, hey there. Nice to see you again."

The Birdperson just cocked his/her/its head. "Busy night," said Merk. The Birdperson continued staring at him. "On the streetcar, I mean…" he continued, lamely.

Merk was sweating now. Maybe The Birdperson didn't understand him? Or maybe he was intruding? Had it been rude of him to speak before being spoken to? Looking for something else, anything, to concentrate on, Merk pulled out a granola bar.

The Birdperson darted across the aisle and "alighted" next to him, pecking at the granola bar, while gently cooing at his cheek. "Wow," said Merk, stammering. "This is… okay… that's nice of you."

"King and Jarvis," said the driver over the intercom. The Birdperson suddenly pulled down his/her/its sweatpants, crapped on the seat (and part of Merk's shoulder) and, rather than exit the door with the other passengers, squeezed him/her/itself out the open window, falling to the ground in a fluttering heap before standing up and ostrich-walking her/his/its way down the street and out of sight.

Dazed, Merk did his best to clean up the mess on his shoulder as an old Italian lady gave him the hairy eyeball from three seats over.

"Atsa why you don't-ah feed-ah dem dirty tings," she tsked.

Vengeful Hank

It was dusk, and when dusk did its thing, Vengeful Hank did his: sat on his porch, ate a raw pineapple, and thought vengeful thoughts.

Vengeful Hank took his time with vengeance, never repeating a venge, because "The name's Vengeful Hank, not Re-vengeful Hank, and don't you forget it!" he suddenly hollered out loud to some imaginary mistake-making asshole.

"Squirrel," he mumbled twenty minutes later when he remembered that squirrel he was going to venge on sometime for some reason he'd forgotten.

Then it was night, and when night did its thing, Vengeful Hank did his: he took off his human skin and extended his tendril antennae to the stars, bathing in their soothing light, before strolling to the beach to eat some villagers.

The Man-Corset

Henry Fooge looked at himself in the full-length mirror of 'Pinch & Cinch Huomo', where he had spent the last hour trying on various man-corsets. Some white, some black, some with sports team logos. But none brought him pleasure.

It wasn't so much that Henry was overweight. He was a large man, yes, but proportional for his height. Of late, gravity had been cruel, and he was becoming pear-shaped instead of triangular like the men in the Charles Atlas comic book ads he'd seen as a child. He'd long outgrown man-spanks, which now did very little to hold him in, and so he'd turned to man-corsetry with an almost fetishist fervor.

He flexed in the mirror. "I'm not sure about this one either," he said. "Do you have anything else?"

"I'm afraid not, sir," said the store associate.

"That's our last model."

"Well, I guess I'll take it..." he said, not totally convinced. But then something caught his eye. He pointed to a man-corset hanging high up on the wall. "Wait," he said. "What's that one?"

The salesman blanched. "Oh!" he said. "That one? That's, um... a floor model... a decoration, really..."

"I want to see it," said Henry.

"Oh, but it's so old..."

"I want to see it!" barked Henry, filled with swelling, unexpected rage at being denied the teeny man-waist he so desired. "*I want to try it on!*"

"As you wish, sir, of course," said the salesman. Trembling, he grabbed a pole hook and took it down.

The corset was made of the finest Egyptian linen, and as Henry put it on, the clasps, stays, and lacing seemed to do themselves. Henry smiled at his perfectly cinched waist in the mirror. And then, as the corset hugged him, a little too snugly at first, and then tighter and tighter, Henry's smile turned first to a frown, and then to a soundless scream, as the sales associate hurriedly ran to lock the door.

Mark Twain

It was 1897, and Mark Twain was practically bankrupt due to a failed investment in a "revolutionary" but ultimately failed typesetting machine.

It was Twain himself who'd said "no man, deep down in his own heart, has any considerable respect for himself," and so it was that he forced himself nowadays into questionable but lucrative employment, be it a European speaking tour, or, as was currently the case – when he was forced to fight a dinosaur.

As he donned his exo-suit (a gift from green-skinned travelers he'd met in Brussels, "probably spacemen," he reckoned) he considered for a moment how unfair to pit him, a thinking man, against a regenerated Jurassic beast that had no idea why all these tiny creatures were peering at it from velvet-lined box seats around the lip of a great pit.

But these foreign businessmen always paid handsomely to see a Man-Dino fight, and that's what they were gonna see tonight. Still, as he was lowered from a crane within reach of the great beast, he wished he could pull a Tom Sawyer and get somebody else to paint this particular fence, which was a snarling 16-foot-tall T-Rex.

He was in little real danger; as soon as it was done tossing him around like a chew toy a couple times, they'd shoot the thing down with half a dozen Gatling guns. As usual, he would feel unease and guilt after the poor thing was killed, and its bones reburied and passed off as genuine fossils.

But that, too, was profitable.

Deep and Delicious

Summer. 1990.

For nearly ten days, newfound twelve-year old besties Bella and Yolanda shared a cabin together at Lake Macktaclackamackanaw.

Every day after dinner, they'd rush back to their cabin to share a secret; a piece of a full, unopened McCain's Deep and Delicious™ cake they'd found under the bottom bunk of their cabin.

They shared a secret piece of secret cake every day as they shared talk of boys, poetry, periods and Ouija boards. They ingested piece after perfect piece of cake, not quite noticing how this cake did not grow stale, did not leak fluid, did not melt in the heat, did not lose a single perfectly engineered feature of its pristine, post-cold-war-better-living-through-chemical existence.

Summer. 2013.

A recently divorced Bella driving westbound

on Toronto's Lakeshore saw the new billboard for Deep and Delicious Cake™. She hadn't thought of that cake (or Yolanda) for years, but when the words "now with better ingredients" caught her eye...

Suddenly, she came online. She pulled over, and found herself dialing a number she didn't know. One ring. Two rings, then...

"Hello?" It was Yolanda.

The cake overlords had succeeded. Yolanda and Bella were going to kill the Prime Minister.

I Know What I Know

"I know how love hurts," he said over the intercom, his voice cracking. He paused to gather his thoughts. "I guess I'm rambling now." And he definitely had been rambling, for the better part of an hour.

"I know how 3D printers work. I know how to change a flat tire. I know quantum physics, I know Susan Powter, I know how to invest money! I mean, look around the facilities, guys. This island is tricked out!"

"But you know what else I know?" he continued, his voice rising. "I know that if you kidnapped the two surviving members of The Beatles; the bass player and the drummer, in other words," and here he made air quotes no-one could see, "the rhythm section, and if you also took the surviving members of The Who, who are the lead singer and lead guitarist, that should make a great fucking band! And you guys have been here a week and you haven't even picked up your fucking instruments yet!"

Sitting unhappily in the cozy breakfast nook, Paul, Ringo, Roger and Pete glumly listened to their captor's ravings. "Now, I'm gonna go for a walk, gentlemen, and when I come back... *I wanna hear a hit record being made!!!*" The squelch and feedback from the P.A. system being turned off echoed across the compound.

The boys sat silently, sipping coffee, till Ringo cleared his throat. "Maybe if I tried something in two-four..."

"Shut up, Ringo!" they all yelled simultaneously.

"Right, sorry." said Ringo.

The Bishop & the Fairy

Across the plains to the west, heat lightning dragged prying fingers across the heavens, sending peels of harbinger thunder pondering towards the city.

The Panther was on the prowl, and Rome, Indiana needed a hero to save it from his reign of terror; a summer crime wave that had known no equal in the mid-west. Tonight, salvation would be served.

A tiny point of light among the fireflies over Sylvan Lake glowed brightly and zipped above the treetops, gained speed and headed towards the city centre. The Fairy had been awakened.

Shafts of light exploded upwards into the night sky, stamping a shimmering white signal into the ominous silver clouds; the Sign of The Cross. From the nondescript, supposedly abandoned basilica at the city centre, organ music barfed out its hallelujah call.

Atop the Basilica, the gargoyle shadows grew longer, and a grotesque, stony caricature of a man in a mitre broke free of its moorings; The Bishop hadn't heard a confession in a long time, and he hungered for repentance.

The Fairy flew to the centre of the Bishop's crozier as he held it aloft. The Bishop's eyes glowed blood red! The Fairy tinkled a nonsensical stream of chimes. "Ah, my old friend," glowered The Bishop. "The night is ripe for confession, is it not?"

Transforming into a murder of stone crows, they flew down the steeple and through the stained-glass window, down the aisle to the confessional, where they waited.

And waited.

For days.

Until Thursday, when The Bishop asked, "The Panther *is* Catholic, isn't he?"

A Hint of Mint

Morose sat in the subway, annoyed. He was late for work, and the car was stopped between stations.

"Mint?" asked a lady standing beside him.

She was dressed in a black cocktail dress, with a matching purse and shoes. She wore sunglasses and held a mint between her teeth.

"Uh, no thank you..." said Morose, noticing uneasily that there was no one else on the car but them.

"Are you sure?" she said, now sitting across the aisle, dressed in a green and brown fur dragon mascot costume, shooting mints out of her left nostril. "They're very good."

"I'm sure they are. I'm good, though," he replied.

"You're afraid it'll blow the top of your head off and shoot your eyeballs out of their sockets."

"Um..." he began, considering her odd but

very specific statement. "Should I be?"

"Mais, non," she said, now in a purple one-piece tuxedo with live ducks for feet, hanging from the ceiling on a trapeze, extending a mint between her fingers.

"Fine." He took the mint. "You promise it won't blow the top of my head off and shoot my eyeballs out of their sockets?"

"Promise," she said, fluttering her eyelashes.

He popped the mint. It blew the top of his head off and shot his eyeballs out of their sockets, just as the train started moving. She plunked his eyeballs into her purse and exited at the next stop.

"Great work," she mused to herself, "if you can get it."

Long Weekend

Hazy blue skies looked down upon the congested lanes of long-weekend traffic snaking their way towards cottage country.

In the backseat of her parents' van, 13-year old Ramper Djolt looked out the window. In the left-hand lane next to them was a rusted out, silver Nissan. It had been dinged up in the rear quarter panel, and the back door window was nothing more than a black garbage bag and duct tape. The driver was a giant potato, and two of its eyes were looking right at her.

Ramper's mouth dropped open. "Mom! There's a potato driving that car!" she yelled, but as she spoke, the Nissan dropped behind them and disappeared among the lanes of traffic.

"Ramper, don't yell when I'm driving, please!" yelled her dad.

"But there was a potato…" Her mom didn't even look at her. "Ramper, stop making fun of people's appearance," she said.

Her dad looked in the rear-view mirror. "God, jerk, wanna just drive up my tailpipe?"

"Just let him pass," said her mom, trying to unfold a map. Ramper's dad signaled to change lanes. "You know we could get a GPS and get rid of those maps?"

Suddenly, Ramper saw the Nissan was now pulled up to them in the passing lane, the driver's potato mouth sneering at Ramper as he drove by. One of its many sprouts steered the wheel, and two others pointed menacingly at its eyes, then pointed at Ramper, before speeding past them.

Her parents were still arguing about a GPS as Ramper wondered why this potato was out to get her? And then she looked down at her half-eaten bag of chips, and realized the horrible truth.

The Deceased

"I didn't know the deceased," began Pastor Anders, "But I'm told he was a good man."

"HA!" interjected a glowering man in the front row. He was, in fact, the only mourner in attendance. The pastor cleared his throat. "I'm told he was a generous man –"

"Riiiight," said the man in the front row. The pastor shifted uncomfortably, but continued. "He goes on today to rejoin his loving wife, Martha –"

"Mehh!"

" – in the life ever after –"

"Pfft."

"Is there a problem, sir?"

The man was surprised to be addressed. "I'm sorry?" he said. "Is there a problem?" repeated the pastor. "Oh, no, Reverend," said the mourner. "You're doing a great job. Please continue."

The pastor fumed a moment, and tried to find his place, but he was too flustered now, and addressed the man again. "I'm sorry but how did you know this man?"

"I don't."

"Then why are you here?" asked the pastor.

"Will there be sandwiches?" asked the man. The pastor stared at him. "No. There will not be sandwiches."

"Oh," said the man, disappointed. "That's a shame."

Annoyed and frustrated, Pastor Anders completed his eulogy, then shut his prayer book with finality. He was about to leave when he noticed the man was holding his hand up. "Yes?" he snapped.

"Can we ride him?" asked the man.

The pastor was flabbergasted. "Ride him? *Can we ride him?!?*"

"Yeah," said the man. "You know. Like a pony."

A moment passed as the pastor considered his next steps very carefully. And later, as they both rode the dead corpse like a pony, the pastor made a mental note to erase the church security tape.

Hitchhiker Games

Niles Portrind flicked his signal light and pulled over to the shoulder. In the rearview, he watched the young hitchhiker pick up his backpack and run up to the passenger door.

Just as the young man was about to grab the door handle and let himself in, Niles hit the accelerator and peeled ahead about 50 feet, leaving the hitcher in a cloud of dust, before he slammed on the breaks. Grinning, he turned to look.

The hitcher seemed surprised, which Niles found even funnier and he grinned and motioned for the young man to try again.

The gag was repeated a dozen more times. By this time, even the hitcher himself was laughing at being the butt of the joke. He'd feign running towards the door, then laugh as he was pelted with gravel kicked up from the tires as Niles pulled away.

On the 13th round, Niles was surprised to see the young man – who by now was laughing hysterically – pull out a shovel, dig a grave, and then bury himself.

Niles watched as the young man's arms – the only part of him not buried at that point – stuck the shovel upright, and then pulled themselves into the earth. Horrified, Niles got out of the car and ran to the dirt mound.

Too late.

"No!" screamed Niles, frantically clawing his way into the mound of dirt, trying to free the young man from his own grave.

Then... his car engine revved loudly. Niles looked up. The smiling, soiled hitcher sat in the driver's seat, motioning for him to get in.

"What an asshole," thought Niles.

Oven Exam

"What's 'Oven Exam'?" asked Tom reluctantly.

This question came moments after the silence that befell the room after Tom's weird cousin Morris had said "You guys wanna play 'Oven Exam'?"

Morris - who insisted everyone address him by the nickname Nardstar - had arrived uninvited (and solo) at this couple's weekend party at the lake, but since Tom was renting the cottage from his uncle (aka Nardstar's dad) he really couldn't ask him to leave.

"Y'never heard of 'Oven Exam'?" said Nardstar, flipping a bottle cap off Tom's head. "You get into the oven and your opponent puts it on broil. You stay in as long as possible. You get out, you lose. Whoever stays in longest dies, but they win, and the loser has to eat the winner. So the loser's the winner!" laughed Nardstar.

"I'm sorry I asked," said Tom, trying to laugh, as his wife Tamara rolled her eyes and went off to bed without a word.

"Fuckin' *funny!*" said Nardstar, pretending to stretch and warm his ass at the fireplace, but really – once again – he was just trying to show off the RUB FOR LUCK slogan he'd ironed-on to the crotch of his sweatpants.

"We're going to bed," said Jen, taking her boyfriend Paul with her. They were the last couple still trying to endure an evening of stupendous Nardstar-brand assholery. Now it was just Tom and Nardstar, but after a few minutes trying to pretend he could do this, Tom caved. "Well, I'm off, too, I guess," he said, and headed off towards his own room. "Wow. Some party," said Nardstar, sarcastically. "Whatever, g'night."

Nardstar sat there, alone, as he always did. He checked his watch. 9:30 pm. He felt sad no-one liked him; almost sad enough to feel guilty about having just roofied everyone. But he knew he'd feel better in about an hour, when he went room to room for a game of "Ghost Lollipop".

Afterlife Wishes

Gary came to, and slowly realized he was hanging upside down. He undid the seatbelt and fell to the ceiling of the car, which of course, was on the ground. Strangely, he felt no pain, and all was bathed in white light.

He became aware of a ticking sound as a pocket watch floated towards him. "Well, well, well," said the pocket watch. "Look who's coming around."

Gary blinked. It wasn't the pocket watch speaking, he realized, but a tiny mosquito holding the pocket watch. "Yes, I'm a mosquito with a human-sized pocket watch," said the mosquito. "Don't judge me. This is _my_ afterlife wish. I wanted a pocket watch and it's my own damn fault I wasn't thinking of scale."

"I'm hallucinating," thought Gary.

"You're not hallucinating," replied the mosquito. "You're dead. We're dead. You slapped me dead when I bit you, then you lost control of the car, flipped and hit a phone pole. Live wires fell on the car and electrocuted you. Me. Us. But I was dead already. Slapper."

"But, but," thought Gary. The mosquito sighed. "Gary, it's the afterlife. You get one wish. I wished for a pocket watch so I have a pocket watch."

A bell tolled in the distance. "It's your turn, Gary. No take-backs!"

"I'm afraid!" said Gary.

"Shh," said the mosquito. "I'll help you. Clear your mind. Ready?"

"Yes," said Gary.

"Just think of what you want... and repeat after me." said the mosquito. "Mosquito-sized smoking jacket."

"Mosquito-sized smoking jacket?" repeated Gary.

A mosquito-sized smoking jacket appeared. "Yoink!" said the mosquito, flying away with the smoking jacket.

"NO! Asshole!" screamed Gary, but there are no take-backs in heaven, and he spent eternity without an anus.

Karl

"Karl, this is a new day," said Karl to himself, out loud, in the mirror. "Fresh start. Everyone's already forgotten about what happened yesterday."

In fact, no one had forgotten about what happened yesterday, when Karl - who really just wanted to be liked-had gone into work and declared it to be "Yodel or Yoghurt Day".

He'd gone office to office, offering his co-workers the choice to yodel, or receive a spoonful of yoghurt to the face.

He'd been sent home early, and told to think about what he'd done.

But today was a new day. He was going to do better. He was going to *be* better. He looked at himself in profile, admiring the Windsor knot he'd finally mastered. "Nice," he said. "Necktie On Your Penis Day, here we go!"

The Last Visit

Miles hadn't visited his grandfather since the operation.

His excuse was that he was busy working two part-time jobs and writing his thesis, but his mother had cornered him at breakfast. "Miles, you should go see him." There was a tone in her voice that made any protest fade away. "He's not going to be around much longer."

And so Miles finally went to his Grandfather's retirement home. And as he checked in at the front desk, Miles realized why he'd been putting this visit off. If he was being truthful, it was because he hadn't wanted to see his Gramps this way, and he felt a lump rise in his throat.

He walked down the long hallway to Gramps' door and knocked. No answer. He knocked again; still no answer. Miles tried the door handle; it was locked. A little worried now, he knocked again. "Gramps? It's Miles." Then, the door opened a crack, stopped short by the security chain. An old face looked out apprehensively.

"Hi, Gramps," said Miles. A moment of confusion crossed the old man's face, then recognition and that warm, wide smile appeared in the middle of his long, white beard. "MILES! I'm so sorry! I was asleep! Have you been knocking long?"

"Yes," said Miles. "Well, that's okay," said Gramps roguishly, fiddling as he tried to undo the chain. "You're young. You've got time to kill. You haven't seen me since the operation! The doctor was amazing! Barely a scar!"

Then the door swung open, and before Miles could even walk in, Gramps lifted up his t-shirt. "See?" And there, held in a gravitationally oblivious fashion by a vintage Playtex bra, were Grandpa's new breasts.

"Not bad, huh?" said Grandpa, grinning ear-to-ear.

Miles hesitated. "Uh..."

Grandpa seemed genuinely hurt. "You don't like 'em?"

Sullen Artists

Cualitro was an aspiring painter who lived just above a storefront along Bloor Street, in the Toronto neighbourhood known as The Annex.

"My main problem," she would tell friends as they sipped cup after cup of the cheap, burnt coffee from Future Bakery, "is a lack of motivation."

Her similarly darkly-dressed friends would nod in varying degrees of agreement, in between pouring themselves another cup of coffee from the self-serve carafes when the cashiers weren't motivated to care, which was always.

Then, when the afternoon shadows grew long, Cualitro (not her real name) would buy yet another canvas with the money she'd saved by stealing coffee and return with it to her apartment. And there, she would spend her evening at home with her real problem; a lack of ability to draw, paint, or doodle.

It wasn't simply a lack of talent.

It was an absolute inability to create art.

Whenever she tried to squeeze paint from a tube, it would squirt around the canvas and hit something else; the floor, the ceiling, the fridge. When trying to doodle with a pencil, it would catch fire before she could join two lines. If she put charcoal to her paper, the sketchpad would crumble into dust. She'd tried colouring books, too, but the crayons would escape from her fingers like balloons, zipping around the room before exploding like firecrackers.

She couldn't see that this gift of destroying art-making tools on contact was in itself a new artform, and never told anyone of her process. But what she lacked in artistic ability, she more than compensated for in pragmatism. And when her exhibit of all-white canvases was sold to the Art Gallery of Ontario, her friends all said she'd sold out.

Two Roads Diverged in a Yellow Wood

Two roads diverged in a yellow wood, and Drank Torsten slammed on the brakes to avoid driving his rental car straight off the road and into a tree.

He breathed deeply to calm himself down. Had he drifted off? It was well past midnight and he'd been driving for hours. He'd decided to check into the next hotel, but this dark stretch of highway had produced nary a sign of civilization for the last hour. And now, here he was, where the two lanes of the east-bound highway suddenly veered off into two separate lanes going in different directions.

He looked at the Hertz Neverlost™ GPS screen.

Typically, there were several touch-buttons to choose from: Address/Intersection, Yellow Pages, Previous Destinations, Local Weather, what have you. But now, there was only one button, in the middle of the screen.

It read simply: TRAVEL BOTH

He stared at it for a minute, and with no other electronic option open to him, he pushed it. "Recalibrating..." said the GPS. And then something extraordinary happened.

Drank felt himself lift out of his body. He looked down and saw himself staring back, wide-eyed. He was simultaneously aware of being both his selves... and the sensation frightened him out of his wits.

He was overcome by an urge to stomp hard on the gas. The car peeled out, and he swerved hard and missed the tree by inches as he roared onto the road on the left. He looked out the window, and he could see his astral projection flying off above the road on the right. Off they went, neck and neck on separate, diverging roads, till the awareness of his other self grew faint, and faded.

"You have arrived at your destination." said the GPS.

A Holiday Inn appeared out of the dark, and Drank pulled in, unnerved but exhilarated. It wasn't till he got to the front desk that he realized his astral projection had his physical wallet.

The Antique Sink

Forrest was surprised on the first morning he washed his hands in his newly installed antique bathroom sink.

He wasn't a huge antique hunter, but for some reason this sink had caught his eye. He was looking for things to add value to his condo before resale, so he'd picked it up. The bowl was marble, with alabaster trim. As it had to be wall mounted, he then scoured the city for weeks to find just the right antique taps to install above it.

This led to realizing he'd have to bone up on home carpentry before roughing out the wall to accommodate them, and then he'd have to redo the tiling. He watched hours of HGTV, and bought home plumbing books.

All told, it was a two-month odyssey, but he was proud of having installed the sink himself. But here he was, a shocked expression on his face; the embarrassingly high-pitched squeal he'd let out still echoing in his ears.

Something had touched his ass.

"Ridiculous," he thought, passing it off as a simple muscle spasm. He bent down to retrieve the soap, but it shot out of his hand like a rocket when he flinched involuntarily as the words 'ghost frotteur' crossed his mind.

He chuckled, lathered up his hands again and dipped them into the sink... and again, he felt hands caressing his buttocks.

He washed his hands in the kitchen sink for a month, eventually selling the condo at a loss, because he was a homophobe, and those ghost hands had just been too grabby to belong to a lady.

Torquil's Cheddar

It was close and firm in texture, yet mellow in character.

It was rich and fine, with a sharp, pungent flavour. And mouthfeel? Oh, it had mouthfeel. It literally melted on the tongue.

It was a block of cheddar, and it belonged to Torquil, as far as he was concerned.

"Mine," he would say, rolling the word around his mouth the way he soon hoped to do to the block of cheddar (which he felt was his) but which sat behind the shop window (not his) with a tiny placard which suggested a price that was many farthings more than Torquil had in his pocket (none).

The shopkeeper rapped the window, startling him. "Oy!" said the shopkeeper. "I've told you before! Stop lickin' and steamin' up my window, see? I'll have the constable after you if I see you here again!"

Torquil gave the shopkeeper as withering a slit-eye as he could manage before trudging across the square. "No one in this town appreciates me," he thought, sadly. "I'm a laughing stock because I'm poor. But one day... one day..."

"Excuse me?" said an elderly voice, startling him out of his funk. "GAH!" said Torquil, while letting out a short, punctuative shart.

An old lady stood before him, holding two packages. "I noticed you looking at the large cheddar in the shop. I bought it and had it cut in two, and I'd like to share it with you if you'll have it?"

Torquil's mouth dropped. His lip trembled. A tear formed in his eye.

Then he punched the old lady in the gut and ran off with both packages, because it was *his* cheddar, and also because he was the biggest dick in the village.

Defensive Driving

And just like that, the car went into a skid, and Ben Creosote's world became a slow-motion slideshow. He instinctually oversteered to the left. The bottle-spin trajectory of the Yaris would without a doubt place the middle part of the car underneath the tractor-trailer to his right.

"Why was I driving this fast?" was the first thought to cross Ben's mind. The second was about his last cable bill.

He heard the blast of the transport truck's air horn. He oversteered to the right. Peripherally, he saw the truck begin to jackknife, and his third thought revealed itself as a vague memory of a piece of banana bread that he'd eaten in University.

His roommate's mother had made that banana bread, and it had been so satisfying and delicious that it had given him an erection. "Huh..." he thought. "Weird."

In the backseat-sized water tank, the Dolphin had awoken from his deep sleep and was clicking and braying like an insane person. The translator

Ben wore around his neck barked out a robotic translation. "What the..? Oh. My. God. We. Are. Going. To. Die."

Their front bumper bounced off the truck, giving Ben an extra second for another thought. "No." said the Dolphin, who was also psychic. "Not... the space bees."

It was their only hope. Ben smashed the "in case of emergency" box below the radio, pulled out the small hammer and smashed the jar of space bees sitting in the passenger seat, releasing a thousand freaked-out space bees that now stung him and swarmed the car, expanding with helium as space bees do.

Their car was lifted out of harm's way, and the 18-wheeler hit a tree and burst into flames. As the space bees burst and died, their car gradually dropped back to earth in the snowy median. "Idiot." said the Dolphin. "We needed. Those bees. They take. Twelve years to breed. Kingpin will kill us."

Ben knew things were grim, and they had to think this one through. He began swiping dead bees off his face. "Dolphin," he said, several octaves higher than normal thanks to the bee-lium™. "Y'ever get a boner from banana bread?"

"No," said the Dolphin. "I'm... gluten intolerant."

The Five Badgers of Skip Stephenson

1987.

June 18th.

Midnight.

Santa Monica, California.

In terms of finding badgers under the bedspread, this was a five-badger alarm. And as Skip Stephenson–former host of late 1970s television show "Real People" – was tucking into bed that night, he suddenly remembered the fortune cookie fortune he'd read last Friday at *Wok This Way*. It had been very explicit.

"You will find five badgers under your bedspread."

Skip learned a valuable lesson that night about the nature of corollary relationships; namely, that when you find five badgers under your bedspread, the reverse is also true.

Inspector Withersby Strikes Again

"This is excellent work," said Inspector Withersby, neatly folding his glasses into their case and placing them in his inner jacket pocket. "But this painting is a forgery nonetheless!"

The guests were aghast. Mrs. Drudgery gasped. The servants' faces blanched. Major Barneswing harrumphed as his monocle popped into his glass of sherry. A chorus of 'wot-wot-wots' rose like motes on the sunbeams streaming in through the drawing room drapes.

Across the room, Yang Yao began slow clapping. Heads turned and a sudden expulsion of disbelief from Mrs. Drake also expulsed her false teeth to the Persian carpet, while the Persian cat in her lap yowled in fury and scuttled to safer haunts behind the couch.

"Well, Mr. Yang Yao," said the Inspector.

"We meet again."

Yang Yao smiled and bowed deeply. Mimsy Penchant huffed as Clive Hornsby chuffed while the maid – anxious to continue eavesdropping – took the silverware and buffed.

Suddenly, Yang Yao threw several tiny throwing stars at the Inspector, who threw up his walking stick in a deft parry, as the stars all found deep purchase in its antique wood.

Yang Yao hissed and threw a smoke bomb! The guests swooned; had the villain disappeared?

But no! Three constables brought in a struggling Yang Yao from the servants' quarters door, through which he had tried to escape. "No escape today, Yang Yao..." said the Inspector, pulling off the forger's fake face for the big reveal. "Or should I say... Felicity Bottoms?"

Miss Thrush fainted away into the Vicar's arms as Felicity stole a kiss from the Inspector. "Why won't you love me?" she whispered in his ear.

"Because I love art more," he said, before they carted her away.

The Raven, Part II

'Twas now long past midnight dreary, I was knackered, bleak and bleary,
Having failed to coax that Raven out the door.
While I plotted, fingers snapping, suddenly the bird was flapping,
As he started rudely crapping, crapping on my chamber door!
"What fresh hell is this?" I shouted, 'Crapping on my chamber door?"
Quoth the Raven, "Here's Lenore."

Ah, distinctly I'm recalling, how my skin was set to crawling,
As Lenore's corpse, stench appalling, burst in through my chamber door.

The blood in my face drained, as she lurched forth to eat my brain!
To the gun rack did I run. Then kaboom! She hit the floor;
I cried "Sweet Lord! I've sent her to her doom!"
Quoth the Raven, "Not so soon!"

Then she stood up, looking wretched! Out of ammo, and dejected,
I ran past her towards the woodshed, where my RPG was stored.
It was then that I remembered: poor Lenore had been dismembered,
By the lake, six days ago, by Zombie hordes.
On the wing appeared the Raven! "Sweet bird, help me!" I implored!
Quoth the Raven; "My name's Gord."

What a time for introductions! "Go to hell!" was my instruction!
And I turned my rocket towards undead Lenore.
As she pitifully came trudging, in my pants I started fudging,
And I felt the Raven watching me as sweat

began to pour.
Then that black bird nipped my ear lobe!
Oh! He was rotten to the core!
Quoth he; "Whatchoo waiting for?!"

So I blasted her to Kingdom Come! Her pieces rained like fishing chum,
And something died within me, at the core.
I had lost a lover grisly, and the dawn's light, grey and drizzly,
Revealed to me what life now held in store.
With a crapping bird to shoulder, and my blood a little colder,
We're now Poe and Raven.
Zombie Hunters.
Evermore.

Death

A love-spurned college freshman in Buenos Aires dangled from a noose tied to ceiling beams in her apartment. Her feet dangled, tears streamed her face, but air was still reaching her lungs, and unconsciousness evaded her.

An aging British rock star, on tour in Japan, looked at his reflection in the mirror and gingerly touched the gaping, bleeding two-inch bullet hole he'd just blown in his forehead as it began to heal itself.

A housewife in Peoria was onto her third bottle of sleeping pills to no avail. A jumper at Toronto's Union Station stood up unhurt after bouncing right off an oncoming train. A supermodel walked out of a burning car she'd just driven off a cliff. A widower who'd eaten rat poison suffered nothing more alarming than diarrhea, which in fact was caused by bad Greek yoghurt.

Governments urged the media, under court order, to cease printing 'rumours' that the death rate had dwindled to zero over the course of three weeks.

And in a small home in Sweden, wires hung out of a ceiling socket. Ten feet below lay Death, sprawled in a heap at the bottom of a stepladder, his neck canted at an impossible angle, screwdriver still in hand.

Fiddler Crab in the Top Hat

"If it's trouble yuh want," drawled the Sheriff, drawing his gun. "It's trouble yuh found."

"Heavens, no, my good man!" stammered the fiddler crab in the top hat, his rostrum twitching nervously as he adjusted his monocle. "Trouble is the last thing I'm looking for!"

"So why you stealin' mah horse?"

The monocle-wearing fiddler crab in the top hat sighed, and explained, for the fourth time today, that he was a traveler from the future; that he needed to borrow the horse to ride across the desert to a quantum singularity disguised as a lone cactus. Here he would stop a marauding band of one-dimensional beings from invading Earth to prevent the rise of American prominence in the early 20th Century.

"Huh," said the sheriff, scratching his whiskers with his gun. "That there story sounds rehearsed."

"Well," said the fiddler crab, "Agreed. But I've repeated myself to three other townspeople today. Time's wasting, Sheriff. Either let me go with this horse... or, I suppose you'll just have to shoot me."

A long moment passed. The sheriff considered. "I ain't never heard no story crazy as this... from a fiddler crab wearin' a fruity hat to boot."

"Top hat, thank you," corrected the Fiddler Crab.

"But if what you say is true... how can I stop you? You take that horse and you SAVE AMERICA!"

And with that, the monocle-wearing fiddler crab in the top hat leapt upon the horse and rode out of town, carapace low to the saddle. And he felt just slightly guilty that – for the fourth time today – he'd fooled a townsperson from Gullible Gulch into thinking he was going to save future America.

For the truth was, all the monocle-wearing fiddler crab in the top hat was going to do (for the fourth time today) was ride a horse to the lone cactus outside of town, where he would eat it.

Knobby Retires

Just before dawn, Knobby Leblanc walked out onto the wharf towards his boat.

His family had owned lobster boats in Shediac for four generations, passed on from father to son, but he and Margie had only had daughters. He wasn't any kind of sexist (he'd tell you himself) but he didn't want the girls working on the boat. They were doing too well in school, and he wanted them to have an easier life than he'd had.

Still, he needed help to finish the season, and maybe then, just maybe, it was time to sell the business. So, he'd put a notice in with Manpower last week for an apprentice to "apply in person before 5 am." And today, it looked like someone had bitten.

"Are you Knobby?" said the man as he approached.

"Yep," said Knobby.

"Awesome," replied the man, blowing on his clasped hands as he shivered with cold. "Very excited! Never been on a real shrimp boat."

"Well, that won't change today, then," said Knobby, already iffy about this prospect. "This is a lobster boat."

"What did I say?" replied the man.

"You said shrimp boat."

The man laughed nervously. "Well, lobsters are just big shrimp, right?"

"No."

"Okay. Well, couple questions. First, how many otters are on board? How many bottles of Sriracha hot sauce? And, finally, let's say, hypothetically, that a man is being stalked by a giant white lobster? How would you catch that lobster?"

"Is this a joke?" said Knobby, irritated. He was about to tell him to go home, when a gigantic wave suddenly roared out of the ocean, lifting itself over the dock, knocking both men down and drenching them to the bone. Knobby sputtered to his senses, coughing up seawater as he sat up... And then he saw it.

Standing above them, eight feet tall, was a gigantic white lobster. Its shell was rough and scarred. Seaweed hung from its twitching antennae, and a foul stench emanated from its mouth. As it rose up on its legs, it gave voice to its fury in a guttural, horrific bellow that nearly stopped Knobby's heart.

"Look out!" yelled the man, pushing Knobby out of the way just as the giant beast brought down its crusher claw, splintering the wood inches from his head.

Scrambling out of the way, Knobby watched as the lobster clacked its way towards the stranger, slapping its tail menacingly against the dock as it cornered him against the side of the boat.

The man unzipped his jacket, and out flew four snarling otters. They leapt at the lobster's exposed swimmerets, teeth gnashing, claws slashing, eyes ablaze. As the leviathan howled at his furry tormentors, the man produced a bottle of Sriracha and sprayed it directly in the lobster's mouth. Now roaring in pain, the lobster swiped at the stranger, missed, and then dove into the water. A trail of bubbles breaking the surface traced its path as it swam to the horizon.

Knobby stood, stunned, watching breathlessly as the otters scurried up the man's pant legs back to their hiding places. Then, like an exhausted soldier comforting the villagers, the man walked up to Knobby and placed a hand on his shoulder.

"Will you help me?" he asked.

"No," said Knobby.

What Do You See?

"Tell me," said the Octopsychologist, holding up a large white card with an inkblot on it. "When you look at this, what do you see?"

The girl on the couch stared at it a few moments. "Dunno." she said.

The Octopsychologist stifled a desire to strangle her with his many (well, eight, at least) tentacles. He smiled instead, which, with his beaky mouth, actually had a horrifying rather than comforting effect on most of his clients. But this client was bored by it, and by everything else in her life. "Is it a unicorn?" he asked.

"No." she said.

"You don't see a unicorn?" he said.

"Not really."

"Not really? So you're not sure if you see a unicorn or not?"

"No."

"When you say 'no', you mean you're not sure if you see a unicorn?"

"No."

"I see," said the Octopsychologist, nodding and scribbling notes. He put on a fur hat and tilted his head to the left.

"And now?" he said.

"And now what?" she asked.

"Now what do you see?"

"A fur hat on your head?" she said.

"Do you see a unicorn?"

"No."

"You don't see a unicorn wearing a fur hat when I do this?"

"No."

"I don't look anything like a unicorn wearing a fur hat when I do this?"

"No."

"I see," said the Octopsychologist, nodding and scribbling notes. From his desk he produced a small jar of spirit gum, which he dabbed under her nose. He then pulled out a fake moustache and placed it on her upper lip. Then he held up a mirror to the girl's face.

"Now," he said. "What do you see?"

"A fake moustache?" she said.

"Do you see a unicorn?"

"No."

"Not a unicorn on your lip?"

"No."

"You're absolutely certain that's not a unicorn on your upper lip?"

"Yes."

"Yes, you mean you see a unicorn on your upper lip?"

"No."

"No, what?"

"No, I don't see a unicorn on my lip."

"And why not?"

"Because it's a moustache."

"I see," said the Octopsychologist, nodding and scribbling notes. He smiled again, more horrifically. "And that's our time. Next week, yes?"

"Whatever, Doctor Syzzlk," said the girl.

As the Octopsychologist shut the door behind her, his smiling beak fell in abject sadness. He removed his glasses and rubbed his tired eyes as a purple puddle of inconsolability leaked unbidden from his ink sac. Feeling stuffy, he slid over to the unicorn and opened it to let in the breeze. He felt the warmth of the unicorn on his face, and he gazed at all the unicorns outside.

The Homonym Strangler

"Pizza!" said the voice on the intercom, giving Haudrey no pause to admit the person buzzing entry into her building. But when the door opened, she found a tall, dark and pizza-less man glowering at her, his twitching hands gloved and hanging at his side.

"My goodness," she said. "You've startled me."

"Have aye?" he replied.

"I'm sorry?" she said. "Did you mean to refer to yourself using a naval affirmative, rather than the first-person singular subject pronoun?"

"Know," he said, walking directly towards her. And at that moment, she did know who he was.

"You're the Homonym Strangler! You're on the news."

"No, ma'am," he said, politely enough for won who meant to murder her by strangulation momentarily. "They don't hang murderers in this jurisdiction."

She blinked, puzzled. "Oh, I sea," she said, finally. "You thought I said 'noose' when I really meant the —"

She had no time for exposition as he lunged directly at her. She threw a spayed in his face, but the neutered female cat barely scratched him before running off. Still, this distraction had given him paws.

"Please," she cried as she ran to her bedroom. "Don't slay me!"

"If I wanted a snow carriage, madam, I would bye won!" he said, racing in behind her. She began throwing shoos at him, but her mere words were not stopping him! Luckily for her, he stumbled on some footwear.

She then ran past him, down the hall and into the breakfast nook, where she hid in the Corn Flakes. But he was a cereal killer, and that was the first place he looked. She ran back down the hallway but stumbled sideways into the door jam, leaving her covered in gooey raspberry spread.

And then he was upon her, his hands upon her neck, but he cot her juggler vein, and he was two clumsy for silly circus tricks, so she was able two reach her purse and pull out a gun.

"Please, miss! Don't chute me!" he said.

"Oh, but I must!" she replied, and pulled the lever to the inclined trough beneath his feat. He fell into the apartment below hers. She was safe at last. But not furlong.

Fruit Bat Pie

If it wasn't one thing, it was another. Artemus had left a fresh fruit bat pie to cool on the windowsill while he practiced playing zither. But on returning to the window an hour later, the pie was quite absent.

"You there, Centurion!" he called down to the street, three stories below. A centaur wearing skinny jeans and playing hackey sack looked up. "Who me?" it said, pointing at itself and looking around.

"Are you a centurion?" asked Artemus. "Is your name Centurion?"

"No."

"Then I must have meant *the centurion over there!*" screamed Artemus unnecessarily, wiggling his pointed index finger to an actual centurion, standing next to Artemus. "CENTURION!"

The Centurion - holding his fingers in his ears with his eyes closed - said nothing. The centaur poked him on the shoulder. "Psst," he said, pointing covertly over his shoulder at Artemus. "Drama."

"Wot?!" yelled the centurion, because his fingers were in his ears.

"What d'you mean, wot?" said Artemus. "Someone has stolen a fruit bat pie from my windowsill! I left it to cool an hour ago and now here it is! Gone!"

"Francis!" yelled the centaur, hands on his hips.

"What?" said Artemus, distracted from his high-volume monologue with the centurion.

"My name," said the centaur petulantly. "Not that you asked."

"Sod off, Francis!" yelled Artemus.

"Oh, that's nice," said Francis, in a tone that conveyed he felt exactly the opposite. "I hope your pie is dead," he added under his breath.

"Why are your fingers in your ears!?" demanded Artemus.

"They are not!" protested the centaur.

"NOT YOU! HIM!" screamed Artemus, neck veins popping.

"AAAAH!" yelled the centurion, cowering to the ground.

"Look what you did with all your yelling! Hope you're happy with yourself!" said Francis, trying to console the now crying centurion. "He only just got back from Gaul, and he's still got shield shock!"

"Right! To Hades with you both!!!" ululated Artemus, slamming the shutters. Seconds later, very angry discordant zithering could be heard.

"He's gone," said Francis.

And with that, the centurion giggled and produced the pie from his loculus, lifting the crust to let all the fruit bats fly out. Then, he and Francis played 'rock, parchment, letter opener' to see which of them got to poop in the pie shell before putting it back on the windowsill.

Just Desserts

Luca Amsler was a banker in Bern who had not been home in a very long time, but when news came from family members that his ailing mother had requested to see him, he put aside old feelings and returned to the small Swiss town where he'd been born.

> Everyone in Malta agreed that Censina Demajo's deserts were the best in the country. From the moistest pie crusts, to astounding tortes, flans, bonbons, sugar cookies and imbuljita, it was said that knives, forks and spoons would ascend directly to heaven after slicing, nay, sliding through her creations.

After holding his mother's hand as she slept, the banker went downstairs, put on his coat and went outside. He crossed the road and walked into the family woodlot he had spent much time walking in during his youth.

> The pinnacle of Censina's works were her custom cakes, created for any occasion.

From succulent layer fillings to decadent cake ingredients, everyone had ordered their occasion cakes from her for decades. And when one spoke of the velvety texture of the fondant, descriptive words became irrelevant. Those who had tasted them simply knew.

The banker had lost track of time; almost in a trance. Lost in thought, he had broken trails in the snow in figure eights around the trees, and night had fallen.

There was also no way to simply describe the delicate beauty of Cesina's almost life-like cake toppers. Intricate wedding scenes of bride and groom in marital bliss, montages of bar and bat-mitzvahs, dad's perfect day of golf, a commemoration of climbing the Matterhorn... there was no montage Cesina could not create, if she were commissioned to do so.

A thousand spotlights seemed to suddenly illuminate the forest, and Luca looked up, startled, but was blinded for his efforts and deafened by a sound of a huge glass dome descending from the sky, trapping him inside. His senses became muted and the fugue claimed him again.

News of the missing banker made international news. The latest creation in

Censina's window—a chocolate cake depicting a lone man walking in circles in a beautifully frosted winter forest was quietly delivered to a safety deposit box.

And, on her deathbed, Mrs. Amsler smiled and passed away.

Late Night Diner

It was 3 a.m. at Stank's 24-hour diner, and Belizabeth thought she'd just seen a man-sized cup of coffee walk into a booth at the far end of her section.

Sure that she had imagined it – she'd been working a double shift, after all – she shook her head, laughed it off, and walked to the booth as she fished the pad and pen out of her apron pocket.

"Can I take your —" she began, stopping mid-sentence as you'd expect, when she saw what was indeed a man-sized cup of coffee sitting in the booth, reading the menu.

"Belizabeth?" said the cup. "It's me. Dad. I'm a man-sized cup of coffee now. I can explain."

The Last One

"Next?" said the bank teller.

A large man approached the counter and, without a word, slid a withdrawal slip over to her. He was dressed in feathers, skins and furs of various animals, and an alarm clock dangled from his golden neck chain. His beard was braided, beaded and dyed in competing hues. Atop his headdress sat a stern, ornately saddled great horned owl, and on that saddle sat a mouse in a fez.

"I am Nangtar, last of the Omniscients!" announced the mouse in a commanding if high-pitched voice. "Fulfill the requirements of this scroll, gold keeper!"

Transfixed on the strange trio, she picked up the withdrawal slip, her eyes darting over the account numbers only long enough to tap them out. The account checked out, and she began counting out the money.

The mouse cleared his throat. "Is it possible to have that in ducats?" he asked. "I'm not fond of the new polymers."

"Uh, no," said the teller, realizing only then that her mouth was still hanging open. "We don't have ducats."

"Also the new artwork is all weird now. Laurier looks more like Trudeau or something."

"I could give this to you in old paper twenties...?" she suggested.

"Yes," said the mouse. "I wish to have the funds in paper!"

She pulled out a stack of older twenties and began counting.

"Ogmire is also quick with numbers," said the mouse. "Ogmire, quickly! Five minus three?" The owl sternly hooted twice, stamping his right foot each time. The mouse held his arms aloft grandiosely. The man applauded exactly four times.

"Four hundred," said the teller, handing over the cash. "Is there anything else I can help you with?" As the man put the funds into a tin cookie box, the mouse cleared his throat again.

"Yes," said the mouse. "I find you comely. Have you any, uh... plans for this evening?"

"Oh, uh..." she said. There was an awkward pause. "Last of the Omniscients..." said the mouse, awkwardly now. "As I said... from before..."

"Yes. I... think I have plans."

"Of course," mumbled the mouse, the cheeks under his fur glowing red. "Presumptuous of me."

Later, in his Yorkville penthouse, Nangtar excused his manservant and owl earlier than usual, preferring to quietly finish his Swiss Chalet quarter-chicken take-out dinner alone. "Keeper of Time, Watcher Of The Threshold, Last of the Omniscients," he chided himself. "And here I am again, alone on New Year's Eve."

He retired to his study to resume work on his memoirs. Then, shortly before midnight, he poured himself a thimble-full of thousand-year-old port and opened the window, that he might hear the celebrations far below. He toasted the new year and then fell asleep fitfully in his chair, blissfully unaware when, hours later, a doting Ogmire would alight beside him, shielding him from the cold breeze with a warm, weathered wing.

Acknowledgements

Thanks to Duncan McKenzie and MKZ Press for saying yes to *Vengeful Hank & Other Shortweird Stories*.

Thanks to Don Ferguson, Sheree Fitch, Colin Mochrie and Peter Wildman, who all had nice things to say about my work (even after reading it).

Thanks to Rob Hawke and Gord Oxley for the notes, the scotch, and the constant encouragement and inspiration.

Thanks to Lindsay Grant, Tom MacKay, Christie Chewka, Claude Cyr, Andreanne Cyr, Phyllis Newman, Phil Byer, Heather Watterson, Gary Pearson, Sam Agro, Kevin Brisson, Nicole Durant, Rob Hornsby, Amy McKenzie and so many more who read early drafts of these stories on my blog. The clicks and likes and comments you made as I posted them on my Facebook feed always made my day.

Thanks to every teacher in school who ever gave our class a writing assignment. Everyone else hated it, but not me, because I was "that" kid.

Thanks to Kevin, my brother, who I totally forgive for the trampoline incident. Not sure why I brought it up just now.

Thanks to Claude, Don, Dan, Pierre, Barry, Dana, Shawn, Tim, Nicole, Nathalie, Terry, Bill and Gerald.

And, best for last, thanks to Leah and Bella. Let's go for a nice, long walk.

About the Author

A New Brunswicker of Acadian extract, Marcel St. Pierre is an improvisor, comedian, writer and producer who now calls Toronto home. He is a founding member and former Artistic Director of The Bad Dog Theatre Company and has performed across North America as a member of comedy troupes like Theatresports, The Second City National Touring Company, the Canadian Comedy-Awarding winning Monkey Toast, The Stand-Ins and the comedy duo Frightwig, whose play PRND21 placed 3rd overall for the 2003 Centaur Theatre Award for Best English Play at the Montreal Fringe.

Marcel is a Promax/BDA Award-winner for his work as an on-air promo writer and producer, and was part of the Gemini Award-winning team that produced CBC Television's The Morgan Waters Show. (Best Youth Program, 2007) As well as writing and producing several episodes of that series, he also played the recurring role of The Assistant. His television writing has appeared on CBC, YTV, The Comedy Network, Treehouse TV and more.

You can follow him @shortweird on twitter, or visit his website www.shortweird.com where you can listen to his Shortweird Radio sketch comedy albums. And while he was actually born on Cinqo de Mayo, despite the sombrero, he has never been to Mexico.

CPSIA information can be obtained at www.ICGtesting.com
Printed in the USA
LVOW10s1745050516

486866LV00020B/807/P